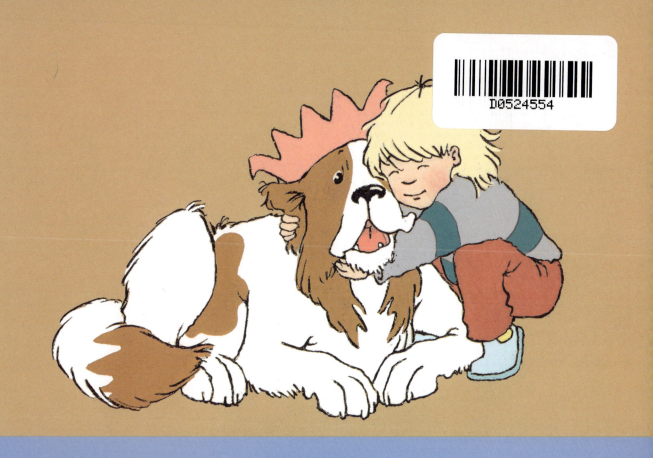

It is Winnie's birthday.

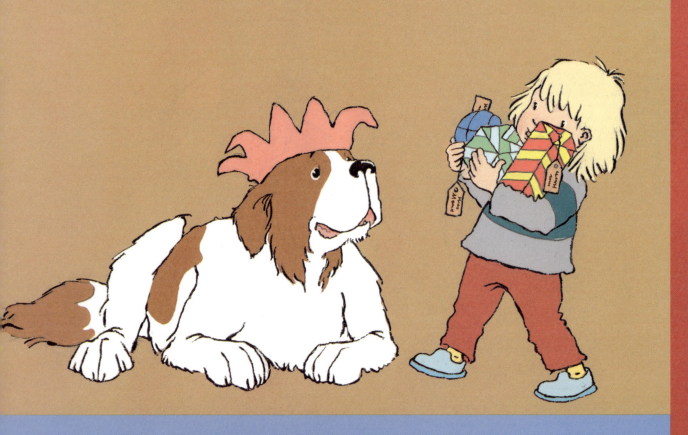

Winnie gets three presents.

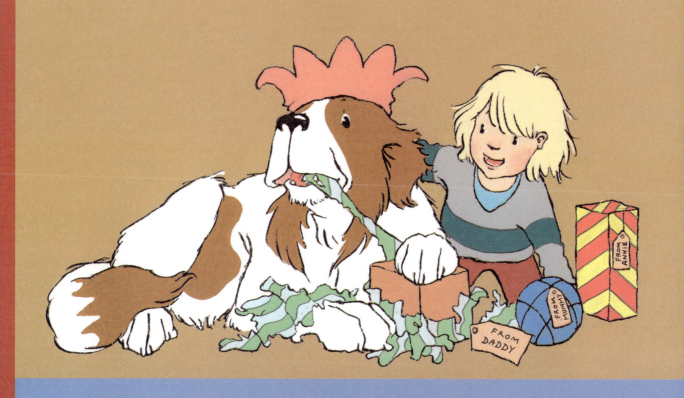

Winnie opens her first present.

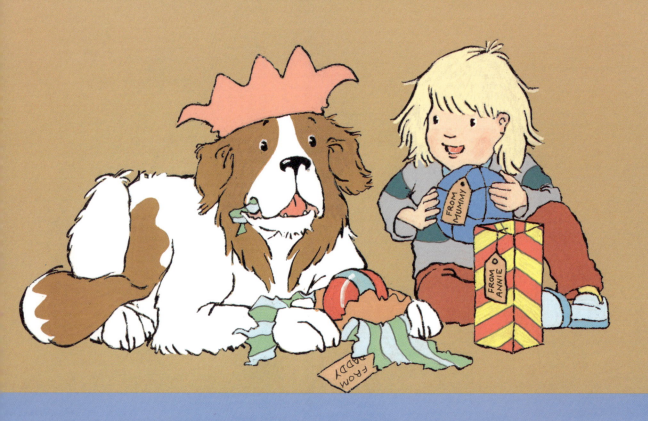

It is a new ball.

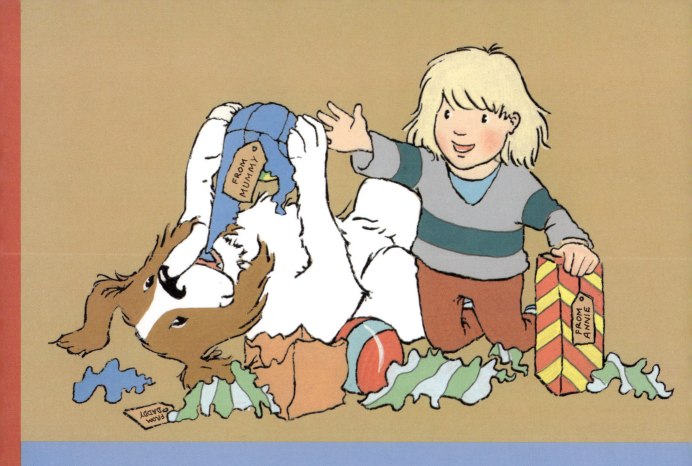

Winnie opens her next present.

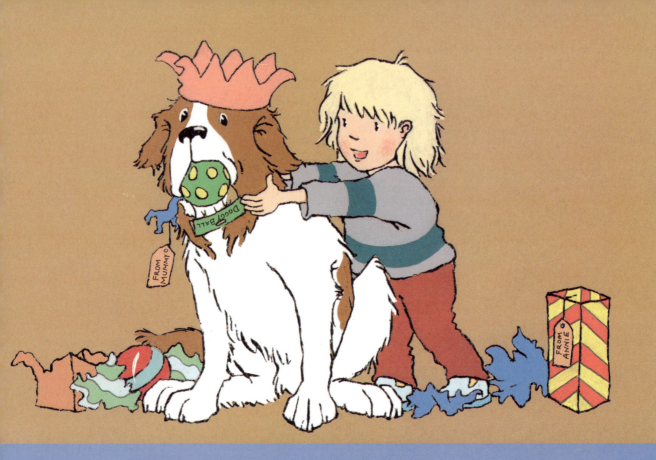

It is a new ball.

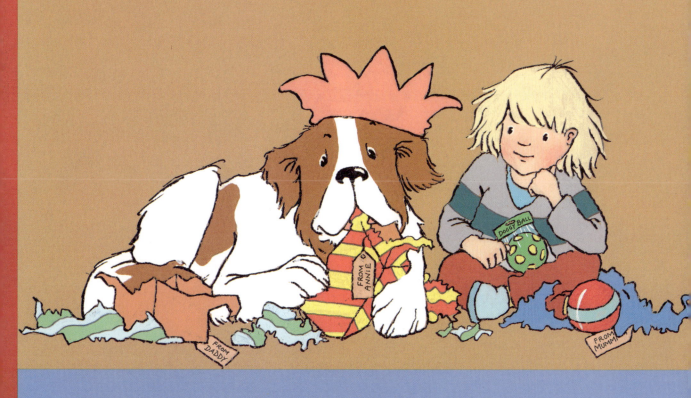

Winnie opens her last present.

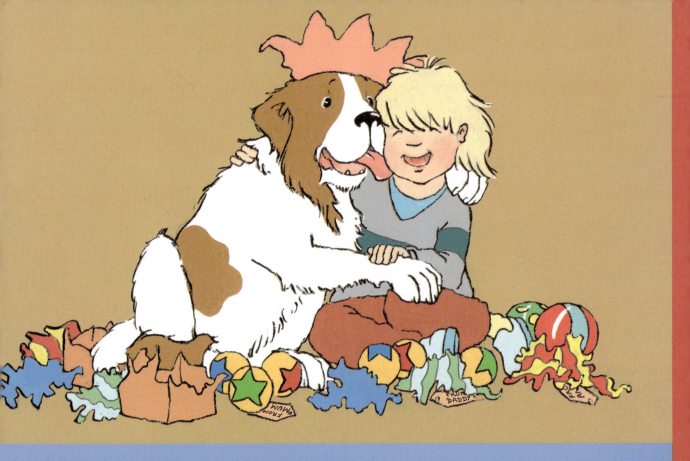

SIX new balls from Annie!